Miss Moo Goes to the Zoo

written by Kelly Graves
illustrated by Liisa Chauncy Guida

SCHOLASTIC INC.
New York   Toronto   London   Auckland   Sydney

Miss Moo lived on a farm out in the countryside. Across the farm, from the barn to the fields, all the animals lived happily together.

But for Miss Moo, nothing exciting ever happened. And without really knowing why—

Miss Moo was very sad.

4

One day, Miss Moo announced to her barnyard friends: "I just can't stay. It's so boring here! I think it's time that I go my own way."

All the animals got together and said: "Oh, Miss Moo! Please don't go. We love you so."

But Miss Moo shook her head, brushed away a moo-tear, and said—

"I have to go!"

And off she went! Soon Miss Moo
came to another farm. She saw friendly
horses and sheep, a hen and her chicks, and a
couple of pigs. They all seemed happy, that was
clear. But she knew that nothing would be
different here.

So she kept walking and walking and walking until—

she came to the zoo.

It was the city zoo. A zoo for Miss Moo? What could she do but walk in and explore?

All of a sudden, Miss Moo heard a strange animal sound. Turning around, she saw—

9

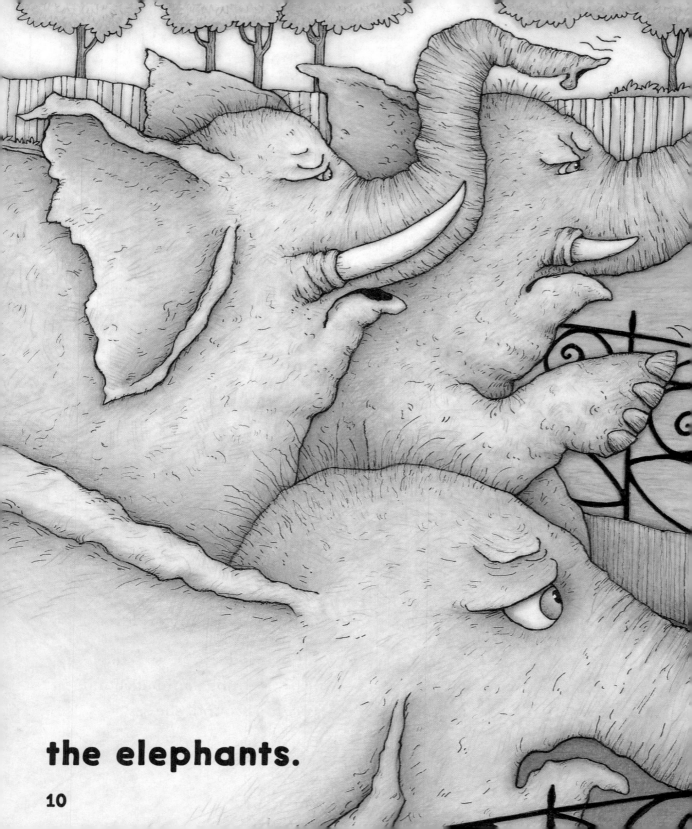

the elephants.

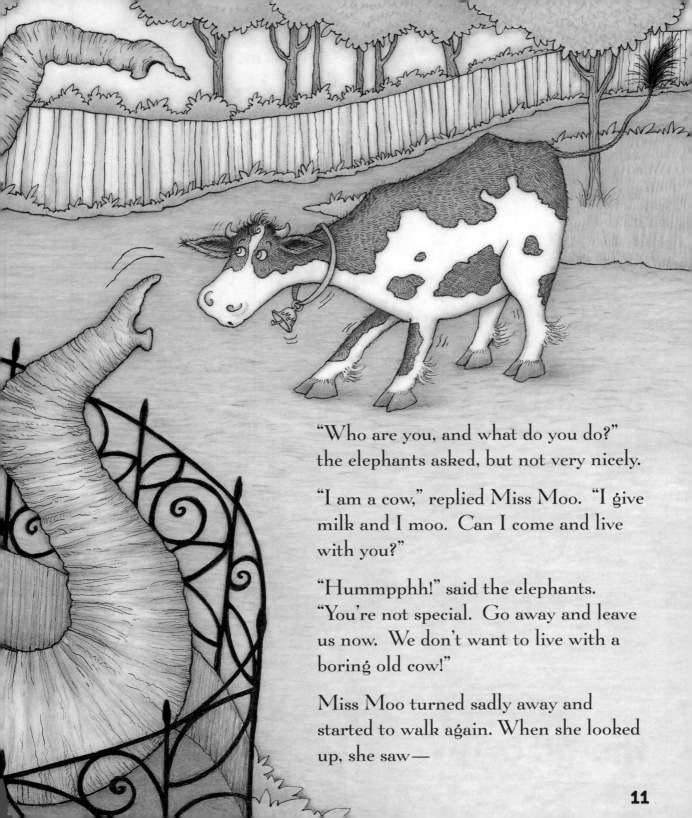

"Who are you, and what do you do?"
the elephants asked, but not very nicely.

"I am a cow," replied Miss Moo. "I give
milk and I moo. Can I come and live
with you?"

"Hummpphh!" said the elephants.
"You're not special. Go away and leave
us now. We don't want to live with a
boring old cow!"

Miss Moo turned sadly away and
started to walk again. When she looked
up, she saw—

the giraffes.

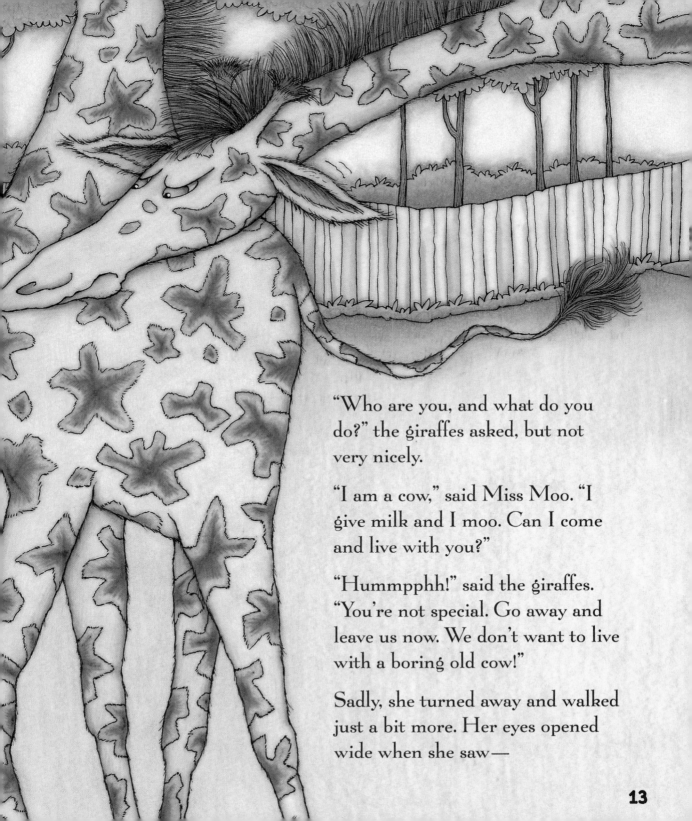

"Who are you, and what do you do?" the giraffes asked, but not very nicely.

"I am a cow," said Miss Moo. "I give milk and I moo. Can I come and live with you?"

"Hummpphh!" said the giraffes. "You're not special. Go away and leave us now. We don't want to live with a boring old cow!"

Sadly, she turned away and walked just a bit more. Her eyes opened wide when she saw—

13

the lions!

"Who are you, and what do you do?" the lions roared, but not nicely at all. AT ALL!

"Oh, dear!" said Miss Moo. "I'm a cow. I give milk and I moo. But I'm not sure if I want to live with you."

"HUMMPPHH!" said the lions. "What's so special about a cow? Go away and leave us—NOW!"

Miss Moo ran all the way to the other side of the zoo. And she began to cry—

"Moooo-hoooo!"

"Who are you, and what do you do?" came a very nice voice from behind Miss Moo.

"I'm just a boring old cow," said poor Miss Moo. "I can only give milk, and that won't interest you."

"Hummpphh!" said the zebras. "Who are we to say? We just stand in the sun and graze all day. But the zookeeper feeds us right about now. He should know what to do with a cow!"

Sure enough, the zookeeper walked right up to Miss Moo and said—

17

"Who are you, and what do you do?"

"I'm not an elephant, big and gray. I'm not a giraffe who stretches tall every day. I'm not even a lion with a great big roar. I'm just a cow who's a bit of a bore."

"Now, Miss Cow, that's no way to talk. Come with me. Let's go for a walk," said the zookeeper.

So Miss Moo followed him to—

19

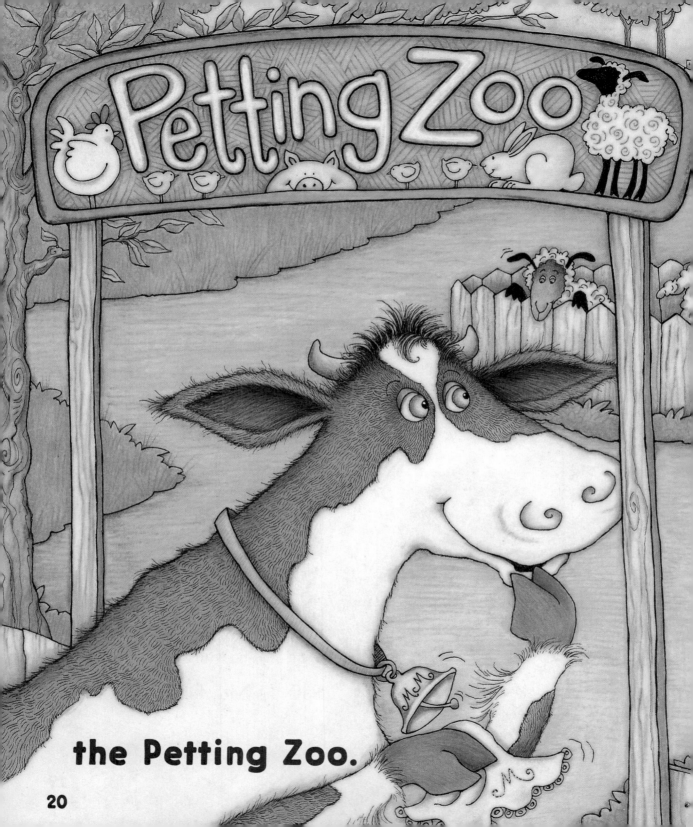

the Petting Zoo.

What a surprise! Miss Moo could not believe her eyes. There were children everywhere, petting and feeding the animals. And these animals were not elephants, giraffes, or lions. They were—

21

pigs, sheep, hens, and horses!

"Miss Moo," said the zookeeper. "Your journey is at end. Stay here with us and be our friend."

Miss Moo stared at all the children. She looked at the animals who lived in the Petting Zoo. She smiled shyly and everyone smiled back.

And at last she knew what she would do. At last there was a new home—

23

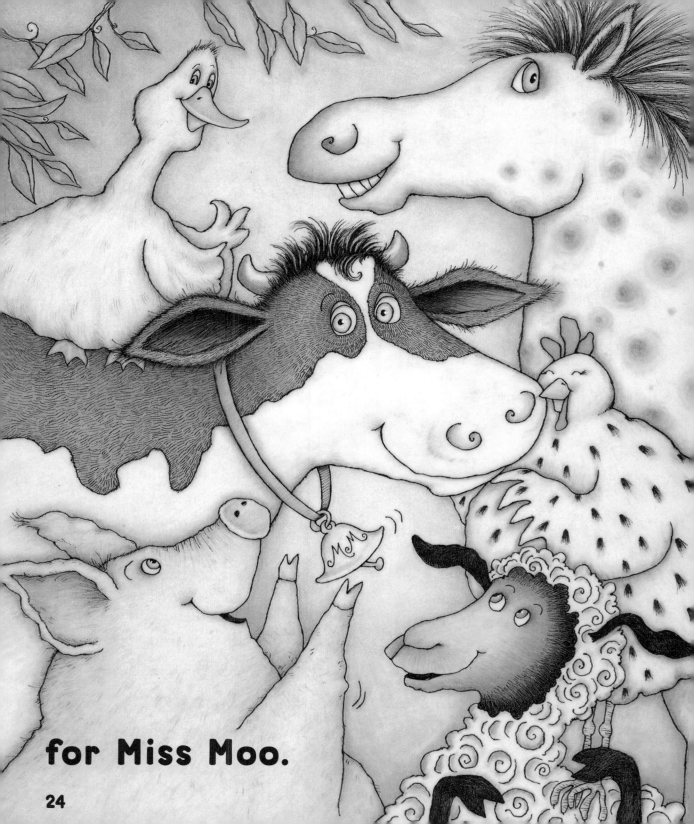

for Miss Moo.